Adventures in Goose Park

Debra Adams

Fulton Books
Meadville, PA

Published by Fulton Books 2023

ISBN 979-8-88731-271-2 (paperback)
ISBN 979-8-88731-272-9 (digital)

Printed in the United States of America

What Do You Know About Geese?

Geese are one of the largest water birds, but they spend most of their time on land. Geese always fly in the shape of a V because it helps the birds to ride the wind created by the wings of their leader.

Geese are very social animals. They are very friendly with each other most of the time. They are also good team players. If a bird is flying alone, he may become tired. It will then join the flock that is flying in a V shape. The birds in front provide extra wind for the tired bird to glide and not work so hard to fly.

Geese are grazing birds that eat a variety of foods. They eat roots, shoots, stems, seeds, and leaves of grass and grain, bulbs, and berries. They also eat insects.

Vocabulary Words

acknowledge. Accept or admit to the existence of a truth.

apologize. Express regret for something someone has done wrong.

benefit. An advantage or profit gained.

complain. To express dissatisfaction.

complimented. A polite expression of praise or admiration.

confess. Admit or state that one is at fault in some way.

confrontational. Dealing with situations in an aggressive or hostile way, aggressive.

defiant. Willingness to contend or fight.

dilemma. A situation in which a difficult choice must be made.

diplomatic. Skill in dealing with sensitive matters or people, tactful.

dishonest. Prone to behave in an untrustworthy way.

expelled. Deprived of membership or involvement in a group.

goslings. Baby geese.

grazing land. A grassy area that provides a healthy diet for grass-eating animals.

hatched. To come out of an egg.

judgment. The ability to make considered decisions or come to sensible conclusions.

lagoon. A shallow body of water separated from a larger body of water.

perceived. Become aware or understand.

reflection. Image seen as in a mirror, looking back on one's own experiences.

route. The way one takes to get to a desired destination.

settle. Get used to a new living space.

urge. To try earnestly to persuade someone to do something.

vulnerable. Susceptible to physical or emotional harm.

welfare. The health and happiness of a group.

wisdom. Having experience, knowledge, and good judgment.

Chapter 1

A Lesson Learned

One day early in the spring, Kiko, leader of a beautiful flock of geese, was flying at the head of the V, the flight formation of the flock. The geese honked happily as they flew high up in the sky over land and sea. Kiko watched below as he flew. He was looking for a special body of water that was surrounded by rich green grass. There, they would find lots of fresh flower shoots, berries, and nuts. Some of the flock might even dive into the water to eat water plants that were tender and moist.

The flock was very loyal to Kiko. He was a good leader and always looked for the best grazing land for his flock. He knew that when the babies would be hatched, they would need to be safe and have very healthy food to eat.

Now among the flock, there was a goose named Tunka. He was very strong, and many of the geese really liked him. He liked to tell jokes and make them laugh. Besides this, when Kiko spotted some good land, before he could tell the flock to fly down and settle there, Tunka and his buddies would race down ahead of Kiko and get the best of the land. That was a problem because the mother geese needed the best of the land to build nests, lay their eggs, and feed their little goslings.

As they were flying one beautiful sunny day, Kiko led the flock over a lovely area that was just right for the geese. It was called Goose Park. You might wonder why it was called Goose Park. It was because the geese loved the fresh moist green grass with mulberry bushes and flower shoots that surrounded the freshwater lagoon where they could drink, bathe, and swim. It was popular with geese, and they always stopped there when they migrated to the North or to the South. Kiko was just about to call to the mothers who were flying near the end of the V. He wanted them to get the best of the land. Before he could honk and tell the moms to fly down, Tunka honked to his buddies to dive down and get the best spots.

Tunka was not a good follower. He did not respect Kiko. Tunka wanted to be a leader like Kiko, but he did not care about the mother geese or their babies. He only looked out for himself.

Kiko was not at all happy when he saw Tunka and his buddies race down to the best of the land. Kiko was concerned for the mothers and babies and had to fly farther to find another area that was good for them.

In the cool of the day, when all the geese families had settled in, and the mom and dad geese had built their nests, Kiko came among the flock. He quietly walked to where Tunka and his buddies were gathered.

"Excuse me, Tunka, may I speak with you for a moment?" asked Kiko.

"Why?" snapped Tunka. "What do we have to talk about?"

Tunka knew that Kiko was not happy with the way he and his buddies took the best of the land from the mother geese. He knew Kiko would deal with him about it sooner or later. This was the time. Kiko invited Tunka to swim with him in the lagoon.

"Tunka, what am I going to do with you? Why do you make so much trouble for the flock? Why do you take the best of the land for yourself when you know all the geese are waiting for me to give the command to fly down and find a good place to settle? Why are you so selfish?"

Tunka retorted, "I'm strong just like you. I should be the leader of the flock. Strong leaders deserve the best of the land! I wanted the best and I got it! If you don't like it, I don't have to follow you. I can find the very best of the land for myself. My buddies will follow me, and we will become a very strong flock. We are tired of you leading us!"

Then Tunka spread his wings and splashed water from the lagoon right in Kiko's face!

He turned and called to his buddies. "Come on, guys! We are not welcome here. I will lead you to even better land than this!" Tunka's buddies called for their families and jumped into the lagoon. They followed Tunka across to the other side. The lagoon was very wide, and they ended up on the side where the ground was muddy and full of weeds.

Tunka's buddies looked around and found no comfortable place to settle down. They found no good food to eat, no berries, and no flowers with juicy shoots. There was nothing but worms and beetles, or they could lick ants off of a giant anthill. None of these were fun foods for the geese to eat. After the little goslings hatched from their eggs, there would be no fresh green grass for them to walk on. The geese families began to complain.

"Why did Tunka lead us here? We had it so much better on the other side of the lagoon. Why couldn't we just stay with Kiko and the other

geese?" They were not happy at all. They remembered that a good leader looked out for the health and welfare of the flock.

"Look, I'm the leader now!" growled Tunka. "Don't badger me with questions. Just do what I tell you!"

Tunka's buddies and their families lowered their eyes with shame. They saw the mistake that they made in following him. After some weeks had passed, Tunka's buddies gathered when he wasn't around.

"What are we going to do?" asked Kaz, one of the buddies. "We can't stay here much longer. Our babies are falling in the mud when they walk, and they're getting lost in the weeds. We're tired of eating beetles and worms. We want the fresh green grass and juicy shoots from plants that grow on the other side of the lagoon. We never should have left there!"

All the buddies put their heads together to figure out a way to return to Kiko and the flock without hurting Tunka's feelings. Kaz suggested pretending to be sick and nothing could help them feel better but the rich grass and shoots on the other side of the lagoon. The other buddies didn't feel that dishonesty was the way out of this dilemma. Lune, another one of the buddies, talked about getting in Tunka's face and telling him plainly that they were leaving, and there's nothing that he could do about it— period! The rest of the buddies thought that was a good way to start a fight. They didn't want to go that route either.

"We will just have to tell him the truth in a nice way," said Ty, another buddy.

"How do we tell Tunka that we don't want to stay with him in a nice way?" asked Kaz.

After much debating the buddies came to an agreement. They would simply tell the truth, but put some nice compliments in it, so Tunka wouldn't feel so disappointed.

"Okay, so we know what we will say. Now, who is going to face Tunka and say it?" asked Lune.

Another discussion arose about who would be the brave one. After all, Tunka was a very strong leader, but his decisions have always been to his own benefit and not for the benefit of others. How would Tunka's buddies help him to understand that other geese have feelings too? They also wanted their wishes to be respected. There was one buddy that didn't really say anything. He just listened while everyone else talked in circles, not really solving the problem. His name was Peewee. The other geese called him that because he was small. Though the buddies would tease Peewee about his size, they had to respect his wisdom. He was very diplomatic when he spoke to others and was careful not to hurt their feelings. Peewee rose among the buddies and declared,

"I will go and talk to Tunka. He somewhat respects my wisdom and might listen to me. I know just what to say to him."

The rest of the buddies were glad that Peewee volunteered to face Tunka because they were afraid to do it.

Early the next morning, all the buddies gathered worms to feed their little goslings and prepared for the swim back to Kiko and the flock. They knew that Peewee would talk with Tunka and explain very nicely that they were leaving him.

Tunka and his family were just waking up when he noticed someone standing in the weeds near their nest.

"Who's there?" called Tunka.

"It's me, Peewee," Peewee answered. "I need to speak with you privately, please."

"Did you have to talk to me so early in the morning? We have barely gotten up and the babies are hungry," said Tunka in an irritated manner.

"It is urgent, sir," urged Peewee.

"Okay then, let's have a little swim in the lagoon. Watch out for the mud near the water," added Tunka.

The two geese swam out for a little space where no one could hear them. Peewee complimented Tunka on his strength and how fearless he was in confrontational situations.

Peewee was careful not to bring up Tunka's poor judgment and how he promised his buddies that he would find them a better place to settle than Kiko found, but never did. He didn't mention that dirty weeds, beetles, and worms were all they had to eat while Kiko and the flock were feasting on fresh, moist green grass with juicy plant shoots and roots. He also didn't mention how Kiko and the flock had a clean, grassy path to the water, but Tunka brought his buddies and their families to a path of mud. Peewee didn't want to make Tunka angry. Instead, he said,

"Tunka, my old friend, we go way back, don't we?"

"Yes, we do," replied Tunka.

"And, we have always trusted each other over the years, haven't we?" asked Peewee.

"Yes. we have," replied Tunka.

"We trusted your judgment when we came here, looking for good grazing land, didn't we?" asked Peewee.

"Yes, you did." Replied Tunka.

"So do you believe that strong leaders with the best of intentions could possibly make mistakes?" asked Peewee.

"It's possible," replied Tunka. "What are you trying to say?"

"I'm trying to say, could it be possible that we made a mistake when we came to this side of the lagoon? After all, we really didn't know that this side was not like the side where Kiko and the flock are nesting. Know what I mean?" said Peewee.

Tunka was quiet for a moment. His mind went back to when the flock was flying all together. They were happy. They were all looking forward to landing in a good place in Goose Park. Tunka remembered how he rushed ahead of Kiko and took the best of the land from the mom geese and kept it for himself. Kiko could have expelled Tunka from the flock, but he didn't do it. Kiko tried to reason with him. Tunka didn't listen. Tunka realized that Kiko was right. If he had worked with his leader, everyone would be smiling right now. Tunka knew in his heart that his buddies and their families were not happy, but he had been too proud to apologize and admit that he was wrong to lead them away from the flock. He made promises that he could not keep. Tunka lowered his head and stared at his reflection in the water.

"Okay, you got me. I was wrong to bring all of you here to this messy place. I was wrong to leave Kiko. Kiko is the real leader, and I was jealous of him. I wanted to lead, but I didn't want to work hard for the flock. I was just wrong."

Tunka sighed with a deep breath. Peewee perceived it was time for some encouraging words.

"It takes a strong goose to admit that he is wrong, and I admire you for that. All is not lost! Just like you humbled yourself and confessed your error to me, you can confess to the rest of the buddies. Then we can all go back to Kiko and the flock together and confess our error to them. We will be together again!"

"It might not be that easy," responded Tunka, "Kiko might not forgive us. He might banish us away from the flock forever!" A tear fell from Tunka's eye.

"It is all my fault! I ruined the lives of all my buddies and their families!" cried Tunka.

Peewee rose up and made himself look as tall as he could.

"As I said, all is not lost. We can't assume that those things will happen. We won't know until we humble ourselves and go back. We can at least try!"

"You are right, my friend. That's why I like you. You are honest and very wise. It's easy for me to trust you! I will do as you suggest."

Tunka gave his goslings something to eat and prepared them for the journey back to the flock. He apologized to his buddies, and they joyfully forgave him. Peewee explained to the buddies and their families what the next steps would be as they swam back across the lagoon. It was a beautiful day, and the water was clear and calm. However, Tunka's heart was racing as they approached the land on the other side.

"I'm still afraid that he will reject us!" Tunka whispered to Peewee, who swam beside him.

"This is no time to be fearful," responded Peewee, being very firm but calm.

Peewee offered to be the first one to step up and face Kiko. He would serve as an ambassador to speak for Tunka and his buddies. Peewee wanted to see what kind of reception Kiko would give them.

Kiko and the flock saw Tunka and his buddies coming while they were a good way off. Some of the geese were concerned. "Is Tunka returning to make more trouble? Will he try to take our land from us?" asked Nebu, a goose that always flew next to Kiko in the V, who stood by him on the bank of the lagoon.

"Shall we prepare to defend our nests, sir?" asked Nebu.

Kiko, being a wise leader, knew no defensive action should be taken without first hearing what Tunka and his buddies had to say.

"Go, tell the flock to stand by their nests. I will stand here and see what they want. If they are looking for trouble, I will honk three times, and the flock should prepare to defend their nests. If they want peace, I will make peace with them. I will honk two times to tell you if there will be peace."

Nebu saluted Kiko and returned to tell the flock. They all obeyed, returned to their nests, and nervously waited.

Kiko stood tall and strong at the bank of the lagoon as Peewee came ashore. "Good morning, Kiko, sir. It's a beautiful day, isn't it?"

"Yes, it is," replied Kiko. "I know that Tunka and the rest of you did not swim across the lagoon to tell me that. What is your mission?"

"With your permission, sir, I will respectfully hand it over to Tunka, who will declare our mission," said Peewee.

Then he whispered to Kiko, "Tunka has a confession to make."

That being said, Peewee went back into the water, so Tunka could step up. The word confession penetrated Kiko's thoughts. No one confesses when they plan to fight. "Confession—what is this leading to?" Kiko wondered.

Tunka slowly stepped up out of the water. This was not an easy task for him. He had always been so strong and defiant. Now he had to be humble and vulnerable. He was at Kiko's mercy. Kaz, Lune, and Ty joined Peewee as they stayed back in the water with the other buddies and their families. They nervously waited.

"Good morning, Tunka," said Kiko calmly.

"Good morning, Kiko," replied Tunka softly.

"So what can I do for you, today?" asked Kiko.

After a pause, Tunka looked up into Kiko's eyes and responded, "You can forgive me."

Since Kiko did not speak to Tunka in an angry manner, he felt free to confess all his wrongdoing and bad judgment. He acknowledged that Kiko was the best leader. Tunka added,

"If you are willing to accept us back in the flock, if you will allow our families to find nesting land among you, I promise to never question your authority again. You have proven your leadership, and I will respect it. I speak for my buddies and their families as well."

A smile came over Kiko's face as he turned around and honked two times. The flock heard, and a sigh of relief sounded throughout Goose Park. Kiko turned again and declared to Tunka, his buddies, and their families,

"Welcome home! We still have nesting space for you and your families. Come, settle your little goslings, and eat the good of the land!"

Once again, Goose Park was a happy place where the geese lived together in peace and harmony.

End of Chapter 1

What Do You Remember?

1. There were two geese with very strong personalities. Who was the real leader among them?

   _____

   _____

   _____

2. One goose was teased for being small in size. What did the other geese respect about him? What was his name?

   _____

   _____

   _____

3. Write a sentence from the story that showed that Kiko truly cared for the welfare of the flock.

   _____

   _____

   _____

Discussion

Read each vocabulary word and its definition.
Relate each definition to a life experience.

Writing Activity

On a separate sheet of paper, choose eight vocabulary words from the list, and write a *complete* sentence for each word. Please connect the sentences to the story, but do not rewrite sentences from the story.

Example: Tunka was not very *diplomatic* when speaking to Kiko.

After reviewing the word meanings above, connect the opposites.

dishonest   confrontational
diplomatic   defiant
vulnerable   confessing

Comparing Personalities

Kiko, Tunka, Peewee, and the buddies had distinct personalities just as we do today. Looking at the personalities listed above, which personalities would you ascribe to each character? Match the characters to their personalities below. If a character has more than one personality trait, use more than one letter. You may use the letters more than once.

1. Kiko   _____   a. dishonest
2. Tonka   _____   b. diplomatic
3. Peewee   _____   c. confrontational
4. The buddies _____   d. vulnerable
                           e. caring

Chapter 2

We Are Family!

Did you know...

Geese families stick together. When a goose chooses a mate, it is for life. The male is faithful and works diligently to feed his family.

Geese like to nest and raise their young in quiet and safe places. They also need a place where there is plenty of food for their families. They always look for a body of water nearby. The water is their protection. If a predator comes near to them, they can fight or swim away. Geese will fight fiercely to protect their babies from animal predators or humans that they think may harm them.

Before you read the story...

Vocabulary Words

Write the words below two times each on a sheet of lined paper. Read the definitions.

accomplish. Achieve or complete successfully.

command. Give an authoritative order.

council. A group of people who come together to consult, deliberate, or make decisions.

crouch. Adopt a position where the knees are bent and the upper body is brought forward and down, sometimes to avoid detection or to defend oneself.

fascinating. Extremely interesting.

forage. To search widely for food or provisions.

frantic. Wild or distraught with fear, anxiety, or other emotion.

intruder. Put oneself deliberately into a place or situation where one is unwelcome or uninvited.

rescue. Save (someone) from a dangerous or distressing situation.

retort. Say something in answer to an accusation, typically in a sharp, angry, or wittily incisive manner.

ruckus. A disturbance or commotion.

It has been the best summer ever with lots of blue skies, balmy breezes, and fruity treats growing in mulberry bushes along the banks of the lagoon in Goose Park. What more could the flock ask for? Kiko strolls through the comfortably nesting families and listens to some of their conversations.

"Tilda, have you laid another batch so quickly? You'll have more babies than any other mom in the flock! When are you going to have time for yourself?" The grandmother geese were concerned that the young moms might wear themselves out from just nesting on eggs every day. Tilda knew that the grandmoms were wise and had lots of experience in raising little goslings. She knew she would do well to listen to them. "Well, Grandma Tori and Grandma Stella, I promise this will be the last hatching for me this year. I'm just ready to go on a nice free flight over the lagoon and beyond the park. I haven't really had the opportunity to see where the humans live. I've been told they sleep in big boxes that light up at night, and they nest there until daybreak. Then they come out and ride on some strange-looking things that roll on something black and round like our nests. I cannot imagine what they must look like. I want to see for myself."

"Tilda, dear, there is no hurry to go where the humans live. They can be very dangerous to the flock. We do not trust them. Humans smile and then throw food at us. We are not begging for food. We have all that we need. I find them most insulting," commented Grandma Stella.

"Why, I've heard that the younger humans will chase our precious little goslings at the other end of the park. One boy human even tried to lure a baby away from his mother. He tried to take him home as a pet. I was horrified at the hearing of it," exclaimed Grandma Tori.

Kiko heard the conversation and concerns of the grandmother geese. He took note of the things he must discuss with the youth of the flock. The dad geese spend time with their goslings, playing games and teaching them how to forage for good healthy food. Kiko knew there was so much more for them to learn.

On the opposite end of Goose Park, there is a playground where young humans like to race and ride on skateboards.

They also like to watch the geese families from a distance. Birds are fascinating to watch, you know. It's all right to watch them from a distance, if that's all that they would do. However, curiosity is one thing that humans are known for, and mom and dad geese know how young humans are drawn to the young geese. More worrisome still, the young geese are also drawn to the young humans.

Over in the park play area, some teens were riding their skateboards. Two young geese happened to be walking nearby when they saw the strange sight of humans rolling around.

"Wow, look at them," exclaimed Lizzy, a teenage goose.

"Why do humans roll around on round things when they have feet to walk on, like us?" commented Ren, Lizzy's friend.

"How about if we take a closer look?" suggested Lizzy.

"I don't know if that's a good idea," said Ren. "Remember the scary stories and how Grandma Stella warned us just this morning?"

"Oh, come on, Ren, are you a goose or a chicken?" retorted Lizzy. "Besides, we know how to fly. If things get a little tight, we know what to do, right?"

"I guess," answered Ren very slowly. He felt a deep sense of *mind your own business* down in his heart. He knew he should insist on taking Lizzy straight back to the flock on the other side of the park, but he didn't like being called a chicken.

"Girly goose? I have a feeling you're going to get us in big trouble," insisted Ren.

"So you are scared," teased Lizzy.

"No, I'm not! I just don't want to do anything stupid. We'll never hear the end of it when we get home," answered Ren.

"It'll be okay, I promise," assured Lizzy, as they inched closer to the skateboarders.

"Well, look what we have here, guys! We got company," yelled Bennie, one of the skateboarders. "Here, goosie goosie" was heard among the teens as they stopped skateboarding to take a closer look at the feathered intruders.

Bennie called for some potato chips to give to the birds. "Put the chips on my skateboard. If the geese get up on the board to eat the chips, we can give them a ride." Yeah, was the response of the group. Lizzy was excited. She had never been so close to humans before. She smelled the chips and drew closer to the skateboard.

"Don't do it, Lizzy," honked Ren. He saw that the teens were setting a trap. "Let's just fly home!"

"Aw, come on, Ren," honked Lizzy. "One chip won't hurt. I never tasted human food before. It sure smells good!"

As Lizzy stepped up on the skateboard, John, another human teen, who was crouched behind her, grabbed her and held her wings so she couldn't get away! There was nothing Ren could do to rescue his friend. He flapped his wings hard as he could and flew to Kiko to get help. Ren could hear Lizzy honking in distress as he flew away. Grandmother Stella's words echoed in his mind as he rode the wind back to the other side of Goose Park. "Stay away from those humans!" Ren was truly sorry that he ignored his better judgment, but it was too late.

It was a lazy, late summer afternoon back at the lagoon. Kiko was helping his mate to do a little nest cleaning since their goslings were now old enough to play in the grass. Lots of geese families were swimming and playing in the refreshing cool water of the lagoon. There was happy honking and joke telling by Tunka and his buddies. The mom geese traded stories while their goslings fed on fresh mulberries. It seemed like everyone was having a perfect afternoon, except for two geese moms who were searching frantically for their teens. Bella, Lizzy's mom, ran from nest to nest, asking if anyone had seen Lizzy. Stella, the grandmother goose, saw her much earlier.

"Wasn't she walking with Ren during breakfast this morning?"

"Yes," said Bella. "I believe so. Oh, where can they be? There's Lea, Ren's mom. I'll ask her."

Before Bella could get the question out of her mouth, Ren came crashing down in the mulberry bushes.

"Heaven sakes, boy, what are you doing and where have you been?" demanded Lea.

"Where is Lizzy? Why isn't she with you?" blurted Bella with a trembling beak.

Ren was quite out of breath, but he tried to answer as best as he could.

"Please! We need Kiko to help us right now!" cried Ren. "They took Lizzy! They got her!"

"Who took her!" yelled Lizzy's mom.

"The humans! They got her!" gasped Ren. He was struggling to catch his breath.

Right at that time Kiko and other leaders of the flock came to find what all the ruckus was about. The flock was very troubled at the news about Lizzy.

"I heard yelling and crying all the way back at the lagoon. What is going on?" demanded Kiko.

"Please, sir," cried Ren, "We've got to rescue Lizzy!"

Those words were very upsetting to Kiko. He prided himself in keeping the flock safe. Now a youth was in grave danger.

"Just tell me where you left her, that's all I need to know," answered Kiko very assuredly.

"Some humans tied her to a skateboard! They're at the playground," cried Ren.

"Son, you did the right thing to rush home for help. Help is on the way. Bella, we will bring back your daughter. Do not worry." said Kiko as he placed his strong wing over Ren. "Call the security guard. Honk the emergency call," yelled Kiko.

The security guard arrived in seconds. "Follow me, my brothers! We have a young goose in great distress. We must find and rescue Lizzy," commanded Kiko.

The troopers ran to pick up speed and soared into the air the way warplanes take off from an aircraft carrier.

In minutes they were circling over the playground. Kiko used his keen eyesight to search for Lizzy.

"If any of you locates Lizzy before I do, just call it out!" yelled Kiko as he flew at the head of the V.

Someone from the back end of the V spotted several teen humans hovering over something on the ground. It looked like a bird flapping its wings. The boys were holding Lizzy by her feet, so she couldn't fly away.

"Why are you so angry, little goose? Didn't you like your skateboard ride?" The boys laughed as Lizzy snapped, honked, and hissed, struggling wildly to get free. Suddenly, very loud honking could be heard overhead. The teens looked up and saw an army of angry geese dive-bombing from the clouds right at them!

Lizzy, freed from her captor's hands, flew upward as the security guard dived down. The teen humans learned that day not to meddle with Kiko's flock. When Kiko saw that Lizzy was free, he called the guard to head home. Their mission was accomplished. There was no small stir when the

32

flock saw Lizzy, Kiko, and the guard flying overhead. Ren was the most relieved of all. He felt that it was his fault that Lizzy was in so much danger.

After Kiko and the guard landed, a council was immediately called. Lizzy, Ren, Grandma Stella, the parent geese, and Kiko. Kiko instructed the young geese to tell what actually happened. He wanted to make sure a near tragedy like this would never happen again.

"It's all my fault," sighed Ren. "I never should have led her over to the humans in the first place."

Lizzy's heart started racing. Ren was trying to take the blame. Should she speak up, or should she just let him suffer the consequences that should go to her? Ren really loved Lizzy. He was trying to spare her the embarrassment of being reprimanded for her disobedience. Lizzy thought it might be okay for Ren to suffer on her behalf until Grandmother Stella stood up and looked sternly at Lizzy. Lizzy's conscience could not take it any longer.

"Kiko, sir and Grandma Stella, I am the guilty party. It was my idea to visit the humans. Ren tried to persuade me to not go. If I had only taken Grandma Stella's warning seriously, I would not have gotten Ren into this mess. I wouldn't be standing here feeling so sorry for what I have done," said Lizzy in a sorry tone of voice.

"Child, do you realize that you could have been killed?" asked Grandma Stella.

"Yes ma'am," replied Lizzy, tearfully. "I have learned my lesson. It will not happen again. Thank you, Kiko, and please thank the guard for me. You saved my life."

The sun peacefully set on another day in Goose Park. All is well that ends well. The flock slept well that night.

End of Chapter 2

Look at the vocabulary list in front of the story. On a separate sheet of lined paper, choose five words and write a sentence about something in the story. Do not use sentences in the story. Make up your own.

Example: Lizzy needed Kiko and the guard to come to her *rescue*.

What Do You Remember?

1. Early in the morning, around breakfast time, what was the first thing the young geese learned from Grandma Stella before they went out to look for adventure?

   _____

   _____

   _____

2. Lizzy and Ren were two teenage geese that heard Grandma Stella's warning. Which one of the two took the warning seriously?

   _____

   _____

   _____

3. There is an old saying. The more something is forbidden to a person, the more the person wants it. In your opinion, is this statement true or false?

_____

_____

_____

4. Do your peers have great influence over you? Y__ N__

5. In your own words, what is the meaning of temptation and how was Lizzy tempted?

_____

_____

_____

6. After being rescued from great danger, what is Lizzy's decision concerning how she will deal with temptation?

_____

_____

_____

7. What would you do if your friends tried to tempt you to do something wrong?

_____

_____

_____

8. In Chapter Two, what words would you use to describe Kiko? Put a check next to the words below that could describe him.

fearful_____   brave_____   unconcerned_____
proud_____   Caring_____   Calming_____
frantic_____   Be prepared to explain your answers.

Meaning of words and phrases: You may refer to the text in the story. What do these phrases mean to you?

- ride the wind
- ignore better judgment
- to dive bomb
- all is well that ends well

There is a saying that says, curiosity killed the cat. How might you apply this saying to chapter two?

_____

_____

_____

Would you allow your good friend to take the punishment that you deserve? Yes_____ No_____.

Tell us why.

Chapter 3

Moving Forward

Did You Know?

Migrating geese return to the exact nesting and wintering locations every year. In fact, migrating geese use various stop-off resting points as they travel—these remain largely the same as well. This means that the geese that you see every spring or fall are probably the same geese that were around your home the year before!

Before you read the story…

Vocabulary Words

Write the words below two times each on a sheet of lined paper. Read the definitions.

appeal. Make a serious or urgent request, typically to the public.

arch. Having the curved shape of an arch.

banquet. An elaborate and formal meal for many people.

confidence. The feeling or belief that one can rely on someone, or firm trust.

contemplate. Look thoughtfully at something for a long time.

declare. Say something in a solemn and emphatic manner.

fatigue. Extreme tiredness.

festivity. Activities or events celebrating a special occasion.

fledgling. Feathers necessary for flight or independent activity.

humiliation. The state of being shamed or disgraced.

scurry. Move hurriedly with short quick steps.

stagger. Walk or move unsteadily, as if about to fall.

"Happy Hatch Day to You" was the song sung by Kiko's flock to all the young geese that hatched exactly one year ago, right in Goose Park. The youth feasted on a banquet of juicy plant roots and mulberries, freshly picked by the grandmother geese. It was a time of celebration as there were lots of yearlings in the flock. While the young geese celebrated growing a little older and a tiny bit wiser, the three-year-olds were paired off, standing by a beautiful tree near the lagoon. The cute couples were not talking about the weather. They were looking in the eyes of their special mates who would share life with them. They were ready to begin families of their own.

Love and excitement were in the air! Lovely and Malik are a notable pair. The flock sees them everywhere together. There's also Amotty and Sarai. They have received blessings from the grandmother geese, Kiko, and the entire flock.

"Don't you just love it, Grandma Tori?" giggled Grandma Stella. "Seeing so many happy geese just makes me happy."

"Land sakes, Grandma Stella, you are telling the truth," answered Grandma Tori. "It kind of reminds me of back in the day when I was a young goosie girl, hee hee."

Over by the lagoon, the hatch day celebrants played water games with their friends as Kiko and Nebu looked on.

"Nebu, I hate to put a damper on all the fun and games, but we must prepare our new fledglings for flight mastery. Time is getting on, and winter weather will be here before we know it. We must take flight and move south to our winter home. If the fledglings do not learn how to fly in time, we will be in trouble. You are a great flight instructor. I will enjoy watching you take on this new class tomorrow."

"It's a pleasure to teach them, Kiko, sir. Watching the goslings stretch out and grow their flight feathers is a great joy. I suggest we encourage early nesting tonight. The fledglings will need to be up right at dawn," said Nebu.

"Sounds good, Nebu. Take care of that for me, will you?" responded Kiko.

"Yes sir!" said Nebu. "All right everyone, we've enjoyed a fun day. Let's get nested early. We've got lots of work to do tomorrow.

In the quiet of the night, along the border of the flock nesting grounds, Tunka, his buddies, and their families were sleeping. Tunka and Ty heard a strange stirring among the bushes.

"What was that?" asked Ty in a whisper.

"Don't know," answered Tunka, also in a whisper. "It's by the bushes. Seems like it's quiet now. Let's go back to sleep."

As the sun rose, the two grandmother geese walked among the nests, honking the wake-up call. The flock was still a bit fatigued from yesterday's festivities, but there was much to do. They dipped in the lagoon for their daily bath and foraged for breakfast.

"I want all fledglings to meet me at the lagoon immediately after breakfast. You must be accompanied by your dads. Thank you," announced Nebu.

As the flock scurried about, one fledgling was not among them. Mokey was still asleep in the nest. The rest of his family jumped up and headed for the lagoon, thinking Mokey was with them. Also, the thing that stirred in the bushes last night was still there, hiding. As Tunka and Ty walked toward the lagoon, the thought about the noise in the bushes last night lingered in Tunka's mind.

"Why don't we make a little detour and walk along the edge of our area, just in case the noise maker is still around?" said Tunka.

"Fine with me," said Ty.

As they walked, they saw Mokey fast asleep in the distance and an orange-looking thing slowly approaching him.

"Well, I'll be a galloping goose feather!" exclaimed Ty "What is that thing moving toward Mokey?"

"Looks like a fox!" whispered Tunka. "Let's sneak up on him before he gets Mokey."

The two crept up behind the predator, and as it was about to put its mouth on Mokey's head, it felt a strong clamp on its fluffy tail. Tunka and Ty bit on the fox's tail with a tight grip.

"Let me go!" cried the fox.

Tunka and Ty didn't bother to answer him. They dragged the intruder far away from the flock. While Ty still had a firm grip on the fox's tail, Tunka addressed him.

"Before we let you go, I'm going to tell you this. If we see your furry face anywhere near us ever again, you will be the first fox ever to try to live without a tail. Is that clear?" demanded Tunka with a stern stare into the fox's eyes.

"Okay, okay, I got the message!" said the defeated fox. He knew he'd better run far before another goose bite ripped his tail clean off!

Tunka and Ty returned to the flock, with their chests' feathers puffed out proudly. They couldn't wait to tell the others what happened. They came to Mokey's nest and found him still sleeping. He never even stirred.

"I don't believe this," sighed Ty. He called Grandma Stella over to Mokey's nest and told her what happened.

"Get up, you bunch of lazy bones and feathers!" yelled Grandma Stella in her best fussy voice. "You almost became breakfast for some old fox!"

Mokey's eyes opened wide when he heard Grandma Stella's voice. He jumped out of the nest and staggered to the lagoon.

Tunka and Ty headed there also. The dads had to help their fledglings do flying exercises in the water.

"Line one, get ready…set…go!" called Nebu as the dads modeled how to wing flap and move along the water. This was the first step. Once the fledglings' wings became strong enough to move them forward, they would go to step two. Step two would teach them how to arch their bodies forward and dip their heads down a bit. That would catch the wind and lift them up into flight. Step three would be taught when they're airborne. They would learn how to extend their wings confidently and command the wind under them.

"Good workout, guys," said Nebu. "Two weeks of daily practice should do it."

Nebu was right. As the second week came to an end, the fledglings were airborne and learning to manipulate directions, ascending and descending safely.

"We don't want anyone to make a crash landing," said Nebu.

Nebu brought the flight training report to Kiko.

"The fledglings are doing well and are on schedule. That is, except for one."

"Except for one?" repeated Kiko.

"Yes, except for one," answered Nebu.

"We can't afford to spend any extra days here in Goose Park. The weather is already changing. Who is it?" asked Kiko."

"Mokey," said Nebu.

"Mokey," said Kiko as his voice dropped. "I should have known. What is his problem?"

"I believe it's a lack of self-confidence, sir. He's strong enough, but he just doesn't stretch out his wings long enough to catch the wind. He gives up too easily," replied Nebu.

"I'll have a talk with his dad," said Kiko as he contemplated what might be done to build Mokey's confidence.

That night, while the flock was sleeping, Piper, Mokey's dad, and Kiko sat by the lagoon and shared ideas that might build Mokey's confidence. One idea was to get two geese to carry Mokey high up over the water and let him go. Of course, falling from such a height would be a failure if Mokey didn't stretch out his wings. His humiliation would be that much worse.

"Let's put an *x* on that idea," said Piper. "How about telling him we are going to leave him behind if he doesn't know how to fly by the time we line up to head south?"

"Now, who is going to tell him that?" asked Kiko. "All the fledglings would go on strike and refuse to fly. They would stay here with Mokey. We have to stick together, Piper."

"You're right," said Piper.

Suddenly, Kiko stood up and declared, "I think I have an idea that will work! You know how the boys like to show off for the girls? If we could get one of the girls to be sort of a cheerleader for Mokey, I believe it would encourage him to fly!"

Then Piper stood up. "How about this, also? We could offer some type of reward for the new flyers. He wouldn't want to miss out on a reward!"

Kiko added, "A reward presented by a cute girly goose!

"Wait a minute," said Piper thoughtfully. "What girl will play up to Mokey? Girls don't even like him. Number two, none of the previous new flyers got any rewards. They might cry 'fowl' on that one. 'Fowl,' get it? Heh heh."

"I've made up my mind. I'm going to appeal to the girls' compassion," said Kiko with resolve.

The next morning, while foraging for breakfast, Kiko casually made the suggestion that the girls show a little interest in Mokey as he attempts to fly and cheer him on. A few comments like "Ew" and "Who wants to like Mokey?" surfaced in the conversation. Then they decided that all the girls would cheer for Mokey together. It worked! Mokey finally got the confidence to hang tough and catch the wind under his wings. There was a great sigh of relief throughout the flock. They won't have to worry about wintering in a Goose Park snowstorm.

By the end of the week, the weather changed for the worse. Pouring rain with hail pummeled the flock. Did they run for cover? No. They stood and faced the storm until it was over. That is what geese do! Kiko's flock has never turned their backs on adversity. They are family, they are brave, and they stick together!

The day finally came for Kiko and the flock to move on. The weather was cool, but the sky was clear.

Kiko gave out the orders for takeoff:

"Okay, troops! Line up in the Lagoon. We'll ascend row by row. Southland, here we come! Row one, let's go. Row two, ready, set, take off. Watch your spacing. Expert flyers stay up front in the V. Females and fledglings take up the rear. Security detail, watch out for eagles. We are on our way!"

The End

What Do You Remember?

1. What does the "Happy hatch day" song remind you of?

   _____

   _____

   _____

2. Why did the geese sing happy *hatch* day?

   _____

   _____

   _____

3. What were the young geese couples looking for when choosing a mate?

   _____

   _____

   _____

4. The grandmother geese prepared a *banquet* for the hatch day celebrants. How do you think the banquet might have been displayed?

_____

_____

_____

5. As Tori, the grandmother goose, watched the festivities and everyone's happiness, she made a comment that sounded like something our grandmothers might have made. Find the comment in the story and write it here.

_____

_____

_____

6. Mokey's life was spared due to the watchfulness of Tunka and Ty. What was the reason that Tunka and Ty decided to take a walk around the edge of the nesting area when they saw Mokey sleeping?

_____

_____

_____

7. Mokey was the only fledgling goose that wasn't passing the flying test. What would you have done to help Mokey work harder to fly?

_____

_____

_____

Choose five vocabulary words and write sentences about the story. Do not use sentences that are in the story. Create your own sentences.

Example: The geese ate lots of good food at the *banquet*.

Open Discussion

Word Meanings

1. Kiko wanted the goose girls to show compassion by cheering for Mokey when he tried to fly. Why were they showing compassion?
2. The story mentions the goose flight class would teach the fledglings to command the wind under their wings. How might a bird command the wind under its wings?
3. When it comes to flying, what do you think it means to hang tough?
4. *Foul or fowl?* Both words sound exactly the same. Look up their meanings on Google search. Reread the sentence where Piper, Mokey's dad, made a joke with the word fowl. Why was it funny to him?
5. According to what you read in the story, what is the difference between a gosling and a fledgling?

Takeaways from the Book

Geese are excellent team players. Flying in the V causes a wind from the flapping of wings. The geese in the front of the V are strong and flap harder. The ones at the end can ride on the wind made from the geese in front. So why do you think Kiko wanted the females and fledglings to fly in the back of the V?

Give an example from the book of the importance of trust.

Why is it necessary to obey wise teaching from those with more experience than you might have? Give an example of the need for obedience, from the book.

Do Grandma Tori and Grandma Stella remind you of anyone in your family? Explain.

About the Author

Debra Adams is a foreign language teacher for over twenty years. She taught students from kindergarten to twelfth grade. After retiring she focused on finding strategies for effectively teaching English reading and language arts to primary students.

Printed in the USA
CPSIA information can be obtained
at www.ICGtesting.com
LVHW071826090224
771459LV00039B/621